Anna, Banana,

and the
Magic Show
Mix-Up

Anna, Banana,

and the
Magic Show
Mix-Up

Anica Mrose Rissi

ILLUSTRATED BY Cassey Kuo

SIMON & SCHUSTER
BOOKS FOR YOUNG READERS
New York   London   Toronto   Sydney   New Delhi

SIMON & SCHUSTER BOOKS FOR YOUNG READERS
An imprint of Simon & Schuster Children's Publishing Division
1230 Avenue of the Americas, New York, New York 10020
SIMON & SCHUSTER BOOKS FOR YOUNG READERS
is a trademark of Simon & Schuster, Inc.
For information about special discounts for bulk purchases, please contact Simon &
Schuster Special Sales at 1-866-506-1949 or business@simonandschuster.com.
The Simon & Schuster Speakers Bureau can bring authors to your live event. For more
information or to book an event, contact the Simon & Schuster Speakers Bureau at
1-866-248-3049 or visit our website at www.simonspeakers.com.
Book design by Laurent Linn
The text for this book was set in Minister Std.
The illustrations for this book were rendered digitally.
Manufactured in the United States of America
0919 FFG
First Edition
2 4 6 8 10 9 7 5 3 1
Library of Congress Cataloging-in-Publication Data
Names: Rissi, Anica Mrose, author. | Kuo, Cassey, illustrator.
Title: Anna, Banana, and the magic show mix-up / Anica Mrose Rissi ;
illustrated by Cassey Kuo.
Description: First edition. | New York : Simon & Schuster Books for Young Readers,
[2019] | Series: [Anna, Banana ; 8] | Summary: When Anna and her friends put
on a magic show to celebrate an elderly neighbor's birthday the grand finale
goes awry, but Banana steps up to save the day.
Identifiers: LCCN 2019001921 | ISBN 9781534417229 (hardcover)
ISBN 9781534417212 (pbk.) | ISBN 9781534417236 (eBook)
Subjects: | CYAC: Magic tricks—Fiction. | Best friends—Fiction. | Friendship—Fiction. |
Dachshunds—Fiction. | Dogs—Fiction.
Classification: LCC PZ7.R5265 Anr 2019 | DDC [Fic]—dc23
LC record available at https://lccn.loc.gov/2019001921

For my favorite Garrisons:
Paige, Cliff, Jess, and Andy
—A. M. R.

For Allie, Mitch, Sarah, and Dani
— C. K.

Anna, Banana,

and the
Magic Show
Mix-Up

Chapter One

The Dragon's Secret

"Okay, my turn to start," my best friend Isabel said. She shimmied on the big rock where we were sitting out on the playground, waiting for the first bell to ring. Our other best friend, Sadie, wasn't there yet. Her bus was late.

"Once upon a time, there was a tiny dragon with a huge secret," Isabel said. She lifted her eyebrows in my direction.

I grinned. That was a great start to a story. Now it was my turn to add a sentence—that was the game we were playing.

I thought for a second. "The dragon's secret was so embarrassing, she hadn't even told it to her best friend the unicorn, or her other best friend, the magic puppy," I said. I almost always put a dog in our stories. Sometimes I even put in my dog, Banana, but not this time. Banana isn't a magic puppy. She's a funny little wiener dog, all long and skinny in the middle, like a banana.

Isabel added the next sentence. "The secret was, the dragon didn't know how to fly."

"Ooh." I liked that. My brain lit up like a sparkler, full of ideas for what could come next. "The dragon hid her secret by pretending the *reason* she never flew was to stay on the ground with her friend, because the puppy couldn't fly either," I said.

If I could fly but my friends couldn't, I would walk with them when we were together. "Magic puppies aren't supposed to fly, but dragons and unicorns *all* know how," I said.

Isabel nodded. "The dragon was afraid that if anyone learned her secret, they would make fun of her and not want to be her friend anymore," she said.

"And she was afraid to practice on her own or take flying lessons at school, because someone might see her trying and failing," I added.

"Also, she was afraid of heights," Isabel said.

I leaned forward and wiggled my eyebrows. "But one day," I said in my most dramatic voice, "the unicorn discovered her secret."

Our teacher, Ms. Burland, says that stories should have a beginning, a middle, and an end. This felt like the start to the middle: the part where things change.

"The dragon and the unicorn were walking to the puppy's house, when the unicorn said they should fly over the mountain to get there faster," Isabel said.

"Hmm." I thought about how the dragon might respond. Would she make up an excuse?

Or create a distraction? I thought she would want to be honest with her friend, but might also feel scared of telling the truth.

"The dragon said no, and when the unicorn asked her why, she started to cry," I said. I waited to hear what Isabel would add next. I had no idea where the story was going. That was part of the fun!

"The unicorn listened carefully while the dragon told him her secret, and he didn't laugh at all," Isabel said. I smiled. Isabel was a good listener too. Almost as good as Banana.

"And then the unicorn told the dragon a secret of his own," I said.

One of the best things about being best friends was sharing—and keeping—each other's secrets. I could always trust Isabel and Sadie with mine. I didn't know what the unicorn's secret would be, but I had a feeling Isabel would come up with something good. I waited.

Before Isabel could continue the story, we saw Sadie running toward us, straight off the school bus. Her backpack bounced with each step.

"You'll never guess what happened on the

bus," she said the second she reached us. She was out of breath from running fast, so the words came out in quick bursts. Her cheeks were pink with excitement.

"You saw a dragon?" Isabel guessed.

"Or a magic puppy?" I said.

Sadie shook her head, still breathing hard.

"I know! The bus driver turned into an ogre," I said.

Sadie dropped her backpack on the ground next to Isabel's and mine. "No! But the driver *did* yell at me, and it was all Justin's fault. He was doing a trick," she said.

"Oh," Isabel said. "Well, that sounds like Justin."

I nodded in agreement. It *did* sound like Justin. He was always making jokes and playing tricks. He could be funny sometimes, but when he was showing off he could also be annoying.

Sadie usually laughed at his jokes and shrugged off his tricks. It was strange for her to be worked up about him. "Was the trick mean?" I asked.

"No," Sadie said. She leaned closer. "It was *magic*."

Chapter Two
Real Magic

Isabel's eyes went wide at the word "magic," but I narrowed mine. I was always suspicious when it came to Justin. "What was the trick?" I asked.

"It was a card trick," Sadie said. "Someone chose a random card from a full deck and Justin guessed what it was. But it was way more complicated than that sounds. No one can figure out how he did it. Not even the fifth graders."

"Hmm," I said. I wondered if I could figure it out. I'm pretty good at riddles and puzzles.

"Do you think it was really magic?" Isabel asked.

Sadie shook her head. "No way. If anyone in our class is secretly magical, it wouldn't be Justin."

I snorted. That was true. If Justin were magical, everyone would know. He would definitely brag about it. A lot.

"Ooh, that's a fun game. Who in our class do we think *would* be magical?" Isabel said.

Sadie tilted her head to one side like Banana does when she's thinking. Her face lit up as she thought of an answer. I kind of hoped she would say *me*, even though I knew I wasn't magical, but instead she said, "Ms. Burland! She would have magic shoes."

I grinned. "Yeah!" Our teacher always

wears fun, colorful shoes. She has the most interesting footwear of anyone I know. The best pair has a kitten face on the toe of one foot, and a puppy face on the other. Those always make me smile.

"She probably knows some magic words, too," I said.

Ms. Burland writes a new word and its definition on the whiteboard every morning—not for a test or anything, just for fun. The word of the day is one of my favorite things about being in her class. Yesterday's word was "optimist." *Optimist: someone who is hopeful and expects good outcomes.* It reminded me of Banana. She's always hopeful that I'll drop her some cheese at the dinner table, even though I'm not supposed to.

The bell rang, telling us it was time to line up

to go inside. Isabel and I slid off the rock and we all grabbed our backpacks. "So how do you think Justin did it? Was it just a lucky guess?" Isabel asked as we walked toward the school doors.

Sadie shrugged. "I don't know. I couldn't really see it. He was sitting a few rows behind me, and when I turned around to watch, the bus driver yelled for everyone to face forward." She wrinkled her nose. Sadie doesn't like being told what to do, even by the grown-ups in charge.

"The fifth graders kept asking but he wouldn't tell them how the trick was done. He said he *guarantees* no one else can do it. So I said he has to show us the trick at recess. I bet we can figure it out." Sadie looked excited. She always loves a challenge.

I felt excited too. "We *are* a good team," I said

as we entered the school. It would be fun figuring out Justin's secret together.

Sadie hooked her arms through mine and Isabel's and we skipped all the way to class.

Chapter Three
You'll Never Guess

When we got to our classroom, I put my jacket and lunch bag into my cubby and went to my seat. I immediately saw Justin, who was already sitting at his desk behind mine. He noticed me looking at him, and grinned. My Nana would say he looked like the cat that had caught the canary—very pleased with himself.

"Hi, Anna," he said. He pulled a deck of cards from his lap and made a big show out of shuffling them on his desktop.

"Hi, Justin," I replied. I dropped into my

seat in front of his and took out my pencils and notebook. I lined up the pencils at the top of my desk—first my regular pencil, then my lucky blue pencil, then my extra-special supersparkly rainbow pencil—and refused to look behind me. If Justin wanted attention, he wasn't going to get it from me. I would *not* be the canary.

But Isabel, who sat at the desk to my right, turned around to see what Justin was doing. "Are those the magic cards?" she asked in a hushed voice, like the magic was sleeping and she didn't want to wake it up.

"Nope," Justin said. "They're just regular cards. It's the trick I do that's magic." I heard the sound of more shuffling, but kept my back to him.

"Sadie said you're going to show us at recess," Isabel said.

"I might. If you're lucky," Justin said. I rolled my eyes even though he couldn't see them. Justin could be so smug sometimes. I wished Isabel wouldn't encourage him.

"Even if I show you, you'll never guess how it's done," he added.

I couldn't stand it anymore. I twisted in my

seat. "We'll see about that," I said.

Justin looked delighted. I should have known better than to take the bait. He pushed his glasses up on his nose and opened his mouth to make some smart comeback, but before he could say anything, Ms. Burland clapped twice to start the day. I turned back around to face the front of the room, and swore I would ignore him for the rest of the morning.

I glanced up at the whiteboard and saw the word of the day: "resolve." *Resolve: to decide firmly on a course of action*, it said. I *resolved* to ignore Justin so he wouldn't know how much I wanted to see his trick. I was betting that the best way to get him to show us how it was done was to act like we didn't care about it.

Luckily I had a lot else to think about besides

Justin. In science we were learning about the three forms of matter: solid, liquid, and gas. But we didn't just talk about them. We did experiments.

First, we melted an ice cube to watch it turn from solid to liquid. Then we heated water until it boiled and became steam—a liquid turning to gas. Next, we did the whole thing in reverse.

We checked the water we'd put in the freezer at the beginning of class, and saw it was turning into ice. We placed a clear plastic cup over a mug of hot water, and observed how the steam trapped by the cup turned into drops of water.

Ms. Burland taught us the words "condensation" and "evaporation" to describe gases becoming liquids and liquids becoming gases. We talked about how water evaporates into

vapor that forms clouds, and clouds condense into raindrops or snowflakes. I liked how when I said the words out loud, they kind of *felt* like what they meant. The word "condensation" plopped like droplets on my tongue, and the word "evaporation" flew off my lips like word vapor.

I nudged my friends and pointed at Ms. Burland's feet. Her boots were covered in clouds and raindrops, with a rainbow on each heel. "Magic shoes," I whispered.

Isabel smiled. "Science *does* seem like magic sometimes," she said.

"But even cooler," Sadie said. Isabel and I agreed.

I didn't look at Justin during the science experiments, or pay him any attention during geography, either. But by the time we went outside for recess, my curiosity was so hot, I thought it might boil over. It was finally time to see the trick!

Sadie, Isabel, and I ran to the merry-go-round. Its flat surface would be good for spreading out playing cards. "Justin! Over here!" Sadie called.

Justin walked up to us and swept one arm through the air dramatically. "Behold!" he said. "Prepare to be shocked and amazed!"

Chapter Four
Pick a Card, Any Card

Isabel clapped. The magic show had begun! I was so excited and curious, I forgot to be annoyed at Justin.

Justin pulled the cards from his pocket and placed them on the merry-go-round in front of us. "Behold," he said again. "A normal deck of cards." We stared at it. It did look normal.

"I will ask the three of you to select one card from the deck," Justin explained in his showman voice. "You will look at that card and memorize it. But don't show or tell me what it is! You will place the card back in the deck, wherever you choose, while I'm not looking. Once the card is hidden, I will use my magic to find it."

I couldn't help it: I already felt impressed. Sadie widened her eyes at me with a look that said, *See?*

Justin motioned toward the cards. "Before you choose your card, do you want to cut the deck?" he offered.

"Yes," Sadie said immediately. She divided the deck in half and placed the bottom stack of cards on top.

"What's that for?" Isabel asked.

"It's to prove I don't have the cards in any special order," Justin explained.

"Oh." Isabel nodded.

"I want to shuffle them," I said. Even though Sadie had cut the deck, it seemed possible Justin still knew how the cards were arranged. If he refused to let me shuffle, we would know that was the secret.

I was certain Justin would say no, but he shrugged. "Sure," he said.

I picked up the cards and shuffled them really well, like my neighbor Mrs. Shirley had taught me. Mrs. Shirley is very good at card games.

Banana and I love visiting her and playing with her and her kitten, Surely Cat. But even though Mrs. Shirley had taught me lots of card games, she'd never shown me anything like this.

The whole time I shuffled, I looked Justin in the eye. I was watching to see if he was worried the shuffling might ruin the trick. He didn't flinch.

I put the cards down.

"Okay?" he said. We nodded.

"All right. I'm going to close my eyes now," Justin said. "Pick a card, memorize it, and place it back in the deck." He closed his eyes. "Tell me when I can open them."

Isabel reached for the cards, but Sadie stopped her. "Will you turn around, please?" she asked Justin.

Justin grinned with his eyes still closed. "As you

wish," he said. He turned his back to us.

I widened my eyes at Sadie and she widened hers back. Justin hadn't arranged the cards and he wasn't peeking. How could he know what card we chose?

Sadie motioned for Isabel to go ahead and take a card. Isabel slid one out from the middle of the deck, turned it over, and showed us what it was: the three of diamonds. We smiled. Good things came in threes—like Sadie, Isabel, and me.

Isabel handed the card to Sadie, who put it back in the deck, near the spot where Isabel had taken it out. I neatened the deck so no one could see which part had been messed with. Then, in a flash of inspiration,

I picked up the cards, shuffled them quickly and quietly, and put them back down. Justin would never know. Maybe the one who would be tricked by this card trick was *him*.

Sadie gave me a thumbs-up. I gave her one back, and so did Isabel. "Okay," Sadie said to Justin. "You can look now."

Justin turned and opened his eyes. My insides fluttered with excitement, like how Banana's eyelids sometimes dance around when she is dreaming an extra-good dream.

"Do you want to shuffle again?" Justin asked, and the fluttering stopped.

My friends and I glanced at one another. "Nah," Sadie said, speaking for all of us. I'd already shuffled, but Justin didn't know that. The three of diamonds was *really* mixed in. It would take some real magic or luck for him to find it.

"Okay," Justin said. He waved his hands over the deck of cards and muttered a bunch of words that were hard to hear but sounded like nonsense. *"Arfer darfer murfer moogs,"* I heard when I leaned closer. The words were silly but his face looked very serious.

Isabel giggled. Sadie shot her a stern look and said, "Shh!"

Justin didn't let them distract him. He kept mumbling the silly words and stayed focused on the cards. He picked up the deck and put the cards down one by one, still facedown, in a pattern I couldn't figure out the logic to. It looked almost like a spaceship. When he got to the last card, he paused for a long moment, said one last magic word, then flipped the card over, faceup. "Is this your card?" he said.

We all looked. Isabel gasped.

"Yes," Sadie said. "But . . . how did you do that?"

Chapter Five

Price to Pay

"Magic!" Justin said. But from his grin, I could tell he was teasing.

I stared at the three of diamonds. I felt dizzy, like the merry-go-round was spinning beneath us, when really it was completely still. How *had* Justin done that? It seemed impossible. Even though I'd shuffled the cards well, I was certain our card hadn't been at the bottom of the deck. It couldn't have been! But there it was, the three of diamonds, the last card Justin had flipped over. I couldn't believe my eyes.

"Wow," I said. I looked at my friends. They were as shocked and impressed as I was. Isabel's mouth hung open, and Sadie was leaning so far forward, it seemed she might tip over.

Sadie straightened. "Do it again!" she said. I could tell she was determined to figure it out.

"Yeah," Isabel cheered.

Justin gathered his cards and knocked them twice against the top of the merry-go-round. "Sure," he said. "If you pay me."

My mouth dropped open too. *What?* I said. That was ridiculous.

"Twelve dollars," Justin said.

"No way," I said. Isabel shook her head, but Sadie seemed to be thinking about it.

"Twelve dollars *each*," Justin added. Isabel looked as stunned as Banana had the first time she heard Mom get the hiccups. (Mom's hiccups were super loud and surprising.)

I crossed my arms. "We're not going to pay you. Just show us the trick again," I said.

"Nope!" Justin said. "You can only see it once for free. Sorry. Stinks to be you."

When he said that, I wanted to scream. He thought he was so smart, just because he knew how to do the trick and we didn't. I wished I could force the secret out of him. But then I remembered my strategy from before. If we wanted to see the trick again, we had to make him *want* to show us. Our best bet was to act like we didn't care about it at all.

I shrugged as if it were no big deal. I couldn't let him know he'd gotten under my skin. "Whatever. We've got other stuff to do right now anyway. Come on, Isabel and Sadie, let's go to the swings!"

I jumped off the merry-go-round and ran to the other side of the playground. After a few seconds, I heard my friends' footsteps following me. They were probably confused about why I'd run away, but I would explain it soon enough.

We needed to discuss and strategize. We *had* to figure out how Justin did that trick.

Chapter Six
Twice as Tricky

When we reached the swings, the bell rang to signal the end of recess. All three of us groaned. I would have to wait to tell my friends what I was thinking.

We walked inside with the rest of the classes, got our lunches, and claimed our usual spot near the windows in the cafeteria. Sadie unpacked her lunchbox and laid the food out neatly on the table in front of her, while I explained my idea about Justin. Sadie likes everything to be organized, even her food. Isabel is the opposite: more messy than neat. She was already halfway through her sandwich before Sadie or I had taken a single bite.

"Hmm," Sadie said when I finished talking. She bit her lip and narrowed her eyes while she thought about what I'd told them: that the best way to get Justin to do the trick again was to act like we didn't want to see it.

"You might be right. Justin *does* like to be contrary," she said. "Contrary" had been a word of the day last week. It means choosing to do the opposite of what's expected. That described Justin pretty well.

"*And* he likes doing stuff just to bug us," I added. Sadie shrugged and bit into a carrot stick. She didn't find him as annoying as I did. She also didn't have to sit in the desk right in front of his.

Isabel swallowed the mouthful of sandwich she'd been chewing and took a sip of her milk. "Don't you think twelve dollars each is a suspicious price?" she said.

I polished my apple on a napkin. "What do you mean?" I asked, and took a big bite.

"I mean, he can't really expect us to give him that much. If he actually wanted to make money, he would charge an amount we could pay," she said.

"Hey, that's true," Sadie said. She spoke slowly, thinking out loud. "He set a price he knew we would say no to. It's almost like that was his way of getting out of it."

I swallowed hard. My friends were right. "It's exactly like that. He tricked us! Twice!" I said. I snuck a glance over at the table where Justin sat, then turned away quickly before he could see me looking. I didn't want him to know we were talking about him.

Isabel dug around in her lunchbox and pulled out a cheese stick. I pictured how eagerly Banana's tail would wag if she saw it, and wished for the millionth time that dogs were allowed in

school. If Banana were here, I knew Isabel would share with her. Everyone would. A dog in school would get so many snacks, she might actually beg to *stop* being fed. Plus, she could help us sniff out the secret to Justin's trick.

"It's weird, because he loves showing off," Isabel said. "So why doesn't he want to show off the magic again?"

"Because if we see him do it twice, we'll figure out the trick," I said. "There must be something that makes it super obvious the second time around."

Isabel pulled a few strings off the cheese stick and dropped them into her mouth. "Maybe he *can't* do it again. Maybe it was just a lucky guess," she said.

Sadie shook her head. "No, because he did

it on the bus this morning, too, remember? I couldn't see it, but everyone was amazed."

Isabel frowned. "Well, if he really doesn't want us to see it twice, acting like we're not interested probably won't work. Sorry, Anna," she said.

I knew she was right. I opened my box of raisins and sighed. Even though Sadie was the most competitive of all of us, I hated letting Justin win. Plus, I really wanted to know how the trick was done.

Isabel jumped in her seat, startling me. "You know what we should do? Go to the library!" she said.

I sat up straighter. That was a good idea. Sadie looked hopeful too.

"We can find a book on magic tricks and look up how they're done," Isabel said. "We don't have to see the trick again to figure it out. We can outsmart Justin on our own."

"Yes!" I cheered. I held up my hand and we slapped a three-way high five. I felt a million times better already.

I hoped Justin was watching.

Chapter Seven

Books Are Magic

After lunch we had math and social studies, then finally it was time to visit the library to check out new books for silent reading. I always look forward to finding a good book, but this week I practically ran through the doors and made a beeline for the school librarian, Ms. Hoyle. Isabel and Sadie were right behind me. They looked just as eager as I felt.

"Ms. Hoyle!" Sadie said. "Do you have any books about magic tricks? Nonfiction?"

"We need three of them," Isabel said.

"Yes, please," I added. I looked behind us to see if Justin had overheard, but he was busy horsing around with our classmate Keisha, and not paying any attention to us.

Ms. Hoyle's lips twitched at the corners. She loved it when students got excited about books. "Why yes, I believe we do," she said. Sadie beamed at Isabel and me. We were in luck!

Ms. Hoyle showed us what section to look in—793.8 in the Dewey decimal system—and we found three books that looked promising: one all about card tricks, and two about lots of kinds of magic tricks. Sadie chose the first one, and Isabel and I took the others. Mine had a whole section on card tricks, but also chapters on showmanship and performance, disappearing objects, and other cool things like that.

I was so excited, I bounced on my toes while Ms. Hoyle checked out my book. I thanked her, turned to the first page, and started reading right there in the middle of the library. I kept reading while we walked back to our classroom and returned to our desks. I didn't stop until the bell rang to tell us that the school day—and silent reading time—were over. Then I grabbed my stuff, said good-bye to my friends, and put my nose back in the book for the entire walk home.

"Don't trip and fall and hit your head," my brother warned as he walked ahead of me on the sidewalk. He waved his arms in the air. "Reading is extremely dangerous! Look out!"

I rolled my eyes and turned the page. Chuck was only teasing, and I was an expert at reading while walking.

When we got home, Banana was waiting for me right inside the doorway like always. She barked and spun in circles to show how happy she was to see me. I closed the magic book and knelt to scratch behind her ears. She licked my chin and I giggled.

"I missed you too," I said. "And boy do I have a lot to tell you."

Banana sat, wagged her tail, and looked up at her leash on its hook beside the door. Her eyes were big and hopeful. "Yes, I agree. We *should* go for a walk. I thought maybe we could visit Mrs. Shirley and Surely Cat," I said.

Banana lifted her ears at the mention of Surely Cat. She loves Mrs. Shirley's little white kitten. And Surely Cat was learning to like Banana, too, or at least to put up with her most of the time.

I stood and let my backpack slide off my shoulders. Dad poked his head around the doorway from the kitchen. He was wearing his red apron that says STIRRING UP TROUBLE and holding a wooden spoon stained with spaghetti sauce. I hoped that was what we'd be having for dinner. "Hey, kiddo. Good day at school?" he asked.

"Yup!" I said. "We did a cool experiment to learn about solids, liquids, and gases."

"You mean the three forms of matter that come out Banana's back end?" Chuck said.

I wrinkled my nose at him. "Gross!"

Chuck laughed. "You should bring her in for show-and-tell," he said.

I put my hands on my hips. "Banana is not a science experiment, and we are *not* studying dog farts," I said. But Banana wagged her tail like she thought it was funny. She doesn't mind when Chuck teases her.

"That's enough, Chuck," Dad said. He turned to me. "If you're going to Mrs. Shirley's, will you ask her if she's coming to the potluck on Saturday?"

"Sure," I said. Once a year, my parents invited all the neighbors over for dinner. We'd put invitations in the mailboxes of everyone on our block, and a few in the mailboxes of farther-away neighbors, too. I'd also invited Isabel and Sadie. It was going to be a lot of fun. I hoped

Mrs. Shirley would join us. She couldn't bring her kitten, though, because Dad is allergic.

I grabbed Banana's leash and clipped it to her collar. "Are you ready to hear all about magic-trick secrets?" I asked. Banana danced at my feet and we headed out the door.

Chapter Eight
Abracadabra

On the way to Mrs. Shirley's house, I told Banana everything that happened at school. When I described how smug Justin got about the magic trick, Banana's ears went flat. When I told her he refused to do it twice unless we paid him, her eyes grew extra round. And when I explained our plan to find the answer to the trick in our books, she at first got distracted by a squirrel running up a tree, but then nudged my hand with her snout to say she thought it was a good idea. Banana is very supportive. It's part of what makes her the best dog ever.

Banana tilted her head to one side, and I knew what she was wondering. "No," I answered. "We haven't found out the secret yet. But I'm only partway through my book, and I've already found lots of other cool tricks. I want to try doing them myself." Sadie and Isabel had said the same thing after silent reading when I asked how their books were. Even if we couldn't learn the same trick as Justin, we definitely planned to learn a few of our own. "I bet I can learn one that's even better than Justin's. Then *I* can be the one to trick *him*."

We rounded the corner onto Mrs. Shirley's street. Banana tugged at the leash. She was eager to see Surely Cat. I walked faster.

"The book says many magic tricks are all about diversion," I said. "A diversion is a distraction the magician creates. The diversion gets the audience to pay attention to something *other* than the tricky part of the trick. Like, maybe she'll wave around a handkerchief or say 'abracadabra,' but the words and the handkerchief have nothing to do with the magic. The point is to get the audience to look at the handkerchief instead of at what the magician's other hand is doing. Isn't that clever?"

Banana swished her tail in agreement. I opened the gate in front of Mrs. Shirley's house and Banana pulled me up the path to her front steps. I rang the bell and a few seconds later, Mrs. Shirley opened the door. Before I could even say hello, Banana poked her nose inside.

Mrs. Shirley laughed. "Come on in, Banana!" she said. She opened the door wider and smiled at me. "You too, Anna. I'm glad to see you both."

"I have an important question," I said. "What do you know about magic?"

Chapter Nine

Magic Memory

"Goodness," Mrs. Shirley said. "That's a big question. What kind of magic?"

I unclipped Banana's leash and she led the way to the living room. Surely Cat was curled up on the couch, taking a nap in a sunbeam. Banana ran over and shoved her nose onto the couch cushion. Surely Cat opened one eye to

look at her, closed it, and continued his nap. Banana's tail went wild with excitement. Surely Cat ignored her.

I slid onto a chair at the table where we usually had tea and played card games. "Magician's magic. Like, card tricks and stuff," I said.

"Oh. I'm afraid I don't know much about that," Mrs. Shirley said. She stepped into the kitchen and returned a moment later with a plate of cookies. "I know a lot of card games but I don't think I know any tricks." She set the cookies on the table and motioned for me to help myself. We each took one, and I bit into mine. It was magically delicious.

"Edward knew a card trick he sometimes did for visitors. He was quite a performer. I must have watched him do it a dozen times, but I never learned the secret. I liked being his audience, and being surprised," she said.

Edward was Mrs. Shirley's husband. He died many months ago, before I met Mrs. Shirley. She talks about him sometimes, and I like hearing the stories. Mrs. Shirley says that as long as we hold on to our memories of someone who is gone, in a way they are always still here with us. I like that.

"I got a book on magic tricks from the library today. Do you think I could borrow a deck of cards to practice with?" I asked. Mrs. Shirley has a lot of cards that she keeps in a special drawer. Each deck has a different photo or drawing on the backs of the cards. My favorite decks are the giraffe cards and the hot-air balloon cards. I always choose one of those when we play together.

"Sure, I'd be happy to lend you one," she said. "You could even take these." She nudged the giraffe deck toward me.

"Thanks. We have a deck at home but Chuck lost eight of the cards from it." I took another cookie. "I won't lose any from the one you lend me," I promised.

Mrs. Shirley nodded. "I know you won't."

"Oh! I'm supposed to ask you. Are you coming to the potluck on Saturday? Banana and I think you should," I said.

At the sound of her name, Banana looked away from Surely Cat for just a second. She barked once. Surely Cat reached out a paw and batted Banana's snout like it was a toy. Banana jumped with surprise, then barked again, this time at Surely Cat. Surely Cat's whiskers twitched with mischief. I giggled.

"Well, in that case, how could I say no?" Mrs. Shirley said. We shared a smile. "Did you know that day is my seventy-sixth birthday?" she asked.

"On Saturday? Wow! We'll have to sing 'Happy Birthday' to you," I said.

"I'd like that," she said.

"What's the best birthday you ever had?" I asked.

Mrs. Shirley shook her head. "Oh, gosh. I'm not sure. There have been a lot of nice ones. What about you, do you have a favorite?"

I thought about it. My last birthday definitely

wasn't my best one. That was when Sadie and I had our biggest fight. We made up later, but it was sad and hard before it got better.

"Hmm," I said. "Actually, my *next* birthday will be my best one because I'll be celebrating with *two* best friends, and Banana." Sadie and I have been best friends forever but we only met Isabel this year. Having two best friends at my next birthday was sure to be twice as much fun.

"That does sound good," Mrs. Shirley said. "Actually, speaking of magic tricks, I thought of a favorite birthday, but it was someone else's, not mine. Does that count?"

"Sure," I said. "What was it?"

Mrs. Shirley took another cookie. "It was a long time ago, when I was about your age," she said. "My friend Eleanor had a party and the whole class was invited. At the party was a magician who performed all sorts of magic tricks."

"Cool!" I said.

"It *was* cool," Mrs. Shirley said. "And very impressive. He did a card trick or two, and made quarters come out of the birthday girl's ears, and turned a handkerchief into a bouquet of flowers."

"Wow!" I said.

"Indeed. But the best trick was at the end of the show, when he pulled a live rabbit out of a hat. It was amazing, and all anybody at school talked about the whole next week." She shook her head. "I still don't know how he did that. It really seemed like magic! I wished and wished for a magician at my next birthday, but my family couldn't afford a party like that. I had nice birthdays, but never one with a live magic show."

That gave me a great idea. I jumped out of my seat, startling Mrs. Shirley and Surely Cat. Banana didn't look startled, though. She knew exactly what I was thinking.

I couldn't wait to get started on my plan.

"I have to go," I said. "Thank you for the cookies, and thanks for lending me the cards. I'll see you at the potluck on Saturday, for sure."

"All right, then," Mrs. Shirley said. She reached down to scratch Banana behind the ears. "See you Saturday."

I gave a quick pat to Surely Cat, tucked the giraffe cards in my pocket, and rushed out the door with Banana at my heels. We needed to get straight to work. Today was Wednesday, and the potluck was on Saturday. There were only three days to prepare for the big surprise!

Chapter Ten
The Magic Plan

Banana and I discussed the secret plan and talked it over with my parents that evening. They were almost as excited as I was. The next morning before school, I told Isabel and Sadie my big idea while we flew back and forth on the swings.

Sadie pumped her legs and flew higher. "Let me get this straight. You want us to put on our own magic show at the potluck?" she said.

"Yes! A surprise magic show, for Mrs. Shirley's birthday," I said. The wind blew a few strands of my hair into my face. I pushed them out of the

way and kept swinging. "She said she likes being in the audience and being surprised, and that she always wished for a magician at her birthday party. We can surprise her and make the wish come true!"

"But we don't know any magic tricks," Isabel said.

"Not yet, but we can learn some. We already

have the books to teach us how," I said. Isabel's swing and mine went side by side for a few seconds as our speeds matched up. She grinned at me. We both loved it when that happened.

"I think it's a great idea," Sadie said. "Let's do it."

We looked at Isabel, who nodded. "I'm in," she said.

"Great." I let my feet hit the ground and drag like brakes to stop the swing. My friends did the same. "We only have two days to practice, but I think it's enough time," I said.

"We'll learn one trick each, but learn them really well," Sadie said. "It doesn't have to be a long show, just a good one. Right, Anna?"

"Right," I said.

"I want to do a coin trick," Isabel said. "Maybe

make one disappear. My book has a few tricks like that."

"Cool," Sadie said. "I'm gonna do a card trick—one that's even better than Justin's. I actually tried some with my mom last night, and they're really fun."

"Perfect," I said. I knew what I wanted my trick to be, too: one that was so amazing and impressive, everyone at the party would be talking about it all week. "I'm going to pull a rabbit out of a hat!" I said.

Isabel's eyebrows shot up. "You are?" she said.

"You can do that?" Sadie asked.

"Not yet, but I'll learn how. It's Mrs. Shirley's favorite magic trick," I explained. The bell rang, so we jumped off the swings and picked up our backpacks. "My book says the rabbit-in-a-hat trick is all about diversion. If I practice really hard, I know I can do it." I loved the idea of a trick that included an animal. I wished I could pull Banana out of a hat, but she was too big to fit in one.

We ran to line up with the rest of our class. "I bet we can find videos of how to do it online," Sadie said. "We'll help you practice. And you can help us practice our tricks, too."

"Great idea! My book says it's also good to practice magic in front of a mirror, so you can see what the audience will see," I said. "It says 'Magic is a performance' and 'Practice makes perfect.'"

"Well, I love to perform," Sadie said. She twirled in a circle with her hands above her head, then bobbed in a dramatic curtsy. Isabel and I clapped.

We followed the line of kids into the school and toward our classroom. "My dad has a top hat I bet he'd let us use for your trick," Isabel said.

"Ooh, perfect. Now I just have to find a rabbit," I said.

"Oh." Sadie scrunched up her face. "Where will we get a rabbit?"

I pressed my lips together. She was right. Finding a rabbit would be much harder than finding a hat. There were wild rabbits in my backyard sometimes, on very lucky days, but I wasn't supposed to touch them. Mom says wild animals like to stay wild. Whenever one saw Banana or me, it always hopped away.

"I have a bunny rabbit," a voice behind us said.

My heart filled up with hope. I turned around to see who had spoken.

The hope whooshed back out like air from a popped balloon.

Chapter Eleven
The Bunny Bargain

We stared at Justin. "*You* have a rabbit?" I said.

"Yeah. Miss Fluffybutt. She's a mini lop," he said.

"*Miss Fluffybutt?*" Sadie echoed. Isabel giggled.

Justin shrugged. "I named her when I was four. And her butt is super fluffy," he explained.

"What's a mini lop?" Isabel asked.

We entered the classroom. "It means she has long, floppy ears that kind of droop off her head. That's the lop part. And I guess 'mini' means she's smaller than other rabbits? I dunno. She likes to eat," he said.

"Awww," Sadie cooed.

Mini sounded perfect! A smaller rabbit would be easier to fit in the hat. "Do you think I could borrow her?" I asked as we walked toward the cubbies. "Just for a couple days?" I didn't love asking Justin for a favor, but it seemed like my only option.

Justin looked suspicious. "What for?" he asked.

"Uh . . ." My brain scrambled for an answer. If I told Justin about our magic show, he might think we were copying him by learning magic tricks of our own. But he wasn't going to lend us his rabbit if we didn't tell him why we needed her.

"We're putting on a magic show! Anna's going to pull the rabbit out of a hat. It's our *grand finale*. That means 'exciting, impressive ending,'" Isabel said.

"She is? No way!" Justin said.

"Way," Sadie confirmed. "Saturday night. It's a birthday surprise for Anna's neighbor."

Justin didn't look mad that we'd copied him. He looked excited. "Can I be in it too?" he said. Sadie's eyes widened.

I hesitated. This was supposed to be *our*

show—Sadie's, Isabel's, and mine. Including Justin wasn't part of Banana's and my plan.

"If you let me be in the show, I'll let you borrow Miss Fluffybutt," Justin said. "But only for Saturday. I would miss her too much if you had her for longer."

I knew what he meant. I couldn't imagine going the rest of the week without seeing Banana.

Maybe it wouldn't be so bad to include Justin in the magic show. The better the tricks were, the better a surprise it would be for Mrs. Shirley. And his card trick *was* amazing. Plus, where else was I going to find a rabbit?

I glanced at Isabel and Sadie to see what they thought. Sadie gave a small shrug and Isabel nodded. It was okay with them if it was okay with me.

I took a deep breath. "Okay. You're in," I said.
I stuck out my hand and we shook on it.

Chapter Twelve

A Magic Solution

"This is perfect," Sadie said once Justin had walked away. "Anna, you're a genius!"

I blinked. "I am?"

"Yes!" Sadie said. But before she could explain what she meant, Ms. Burland clapped twice and we ran to our seats. It was time to start the day.

I took out my pencils and lined them up on my desk, and wondered what Sadie could be talking about. She swiveled in her chair two rows over and one row up from mine, and

gave me a thumbs-up. I widened my eyes and shrugged to show I didn't get it.

Sadie thinks Justin is more funny than annoying, but there was no reason for her to be so pleased about including him in the show. At least, no reason I could think of. Maybe she was just glad we'd found a rabbit.

I looked over at Isabel. She was drawing a fluffy-tailed bunny in her notebook. The bunny was eating a four-leaf clover.

Ms. Burland asked Amanda and Timothy to hand out our geography worksheets. While they were walking up and down the aisles, Sadie turned again and handed a note to Isabel. Isabel passed it to me.

I dropped the note into my lap before our teacher could see it, and unfolded it inside my desk. I cupped my hand over the words in case Justin was peeking over my shoulder.

Sadie had written a line of exclamation points, followed by: *Now we get to see the trick again. You did it! Just like the word of the day says.*

I looked up at the whiteboard and felt confused: The word of the day was "resolve."

But that was yesterday's word! Had Ms. Burland forgotten to change it?

I was about to raise my hand and tell her, when I looked closer and realized she *had* changed it. It was the same word, but with a different definition. It turns out "resolve" has more than one meaning.

Resolve, it said. *To find a solution to a problem or fight.* Sadie was right. I had resolved our problem of how to find a rabbit, and at the same time, I accidentally resolved the challenge of how to see Justin's trick again, too. I guessed he'd gotten so excited about performing it for a real audience, he'd forgotten that meant we would see it again. Or maybe we'd really fooled him into thinking we didn't care how it was done.

I'd tricked the trickster without even trying. Ha!

I grabbed my supersparkly rainbow pencil from its spot at the top of my desk. Being careful to keep the note hidden from Ms. Burland and Justin, I drew a smiley face below Sadie's "P.S." The "P.S." said, *I'm making a list. Discuss at recess!*

I refolded the note and passed it to Isabel so she could see too.

At recess, we ran to claim the swings again but some other kids got there before us. We walked to the reading rock instead, and sat on the ground beside it, since the rock isn't large enough for three. Sadie opened her notebook. "What's the list of?" Isabel asked.

Sadie clicked her pen. "I wrote down all the

ways my book says card tricks can work," she said.

"Good thinking," I said. "If we know how *other* magic tricks work, we might know what to look for when Justin does his."

"Exactly," Sadie said. "This will help us figure out the secret to the magic."

Chapter Thirteen
Magic or Math?

"What's on the list?" Isabel asked. She scooted closer to Sadie and peered at the notebook. I did too.

"First is 'marked cards,'" Sadie said. "That's when the backs of the cards are marked with secret symbols, so you know what's on the front without looking. I don't think that's what Justin did, since he didn't even see us choose our card. But I put it on the list anyway."

Isabel and I nodded. It was smart of Sadie to list every possibility, just in case.

"Next is 'sign from a helper.' That's if you have a magician's assistant or a spy in the audience who knows what the card is and gives you a secret hint, like a hand signal or code word," Sadie said. She narrowed her eyes and pointed a finger at Isabel and me. "Heeeeey, did you tell Justin our card?" she said. Her voice was like a cartoon detective figuring out the case.

I played along. "Oh no! You caught me!" I said. We all giggled. That clearly wasn't the answer. And no one else had been nearby when Justin did the trick.

Isabel read the next thing on the list. "'Prearranged deck.' My book has some tricks like that too, where the cards are arranged in a certain order before you start. There's one where you put all the red cards together and all the black cards together. The trick is, you split the deck into two piles and have someone take a card from one pile and put it in the other pile. Then you pretend to do all kinds of magical things to help you figure it out. But you'll know immediately which card it is because it will be the only red card or only black card in that half of the deck."

"That's sneaky," I said. "But Justin let us shuffle before the trick started. He couldn't have had the cards in order. I mixed them really well!"

"We know you did," Sadie said.

I leaned over to look at the last thing on the list. "'Pattern or math.' What's that?" I said.

"Those tricks are my favorites," Sadie said. I wasn't surprised. Sadie loves math. Her brain is really good at it. "You lay down the cards in a pattern, and the pattern helps you figure out what the card is. I tried one from my book last night that works really well. It seems like magic but it's actually math. I wish I had cards so I could show you."

"Wait! I bet I can make some appear." I reached into the pocket of my sweatshirt and pulled out Mrs. Shirley's giraffe cards. I was glad I had them with me. "Ta-da!" I said.

Isabel clapped at my "magic trick." Sadie reached for the cards. "Perfect!" she said. She slid off the rubber band that was holding the deck together. "Okay, so for this trick I only need twenty-one cards. I'm going to put them in three rows of seven."

Isabel and I watched as Sadie laid the cards down, face up. When they were all in position, she looked at me. "Anna, pick a card and memorize what it is, but don't say it out loud."

"Can she whisper it to me?" Isabel asked.

"Okay, but do it softly so I can't hear what it is. I'll plug my ears and hum," Sadie said. She stuck her fingers in her ears and hummed "Old MacDonald Had a Farm."

I moved over next to Isabel and whispered, "Queen of spades."

Sadie unplugged her ears. "Got it?" We nodded. "Good. Now tell me which row—one, two, or three—the card is in."

"Two," Isabel and I said together.

Sadie picked up the cards one by one and put them down again in three new rows. "What row is the card in now?" she asked.

I looked for it. "The first one," I told her.

Sadie picked up the cards again, made another three rows, and asked which one my card was in. "Row three," I said.

"Hmm," she said. She waved her hands over the cards as if she could feel through her palms which one might be mine. "Abracadabra, hocus-pocus, jazaam, jazoom! Is this your card?" She picked up the queen of spades.

I stared at her. "It is! How did you know that?"

"Magic!" she said, and grinned. "Just kidding. Whatever row you said your card was in, I picked that row up second each time. That put the cards into an order that meant, at the end, your card would be the center card in its row. It works that way every time. It's not magic, it's a pattern."

"Wow!" Isabel said at the same time I said, "Cool!"

Sadie beamed. "I'm thinking I'll do that one at our magic show. I just have to practice it a bunch of times, so no one can see that I'm counting where the cards go. And so it doesn't look obvious that I'm picking them up in a certain order."

"I'll start practicing my coin trick tonight, too," Isabel said. "I bet at least one of my sisters would be willing to be the audience."

"I'm going to practice for Banana and in front of a mirror," I said. "I'll use a stuffed animal since I can't practice with Miss Fluffybutt."

"Good idea," Sadie said. "And you guys

should come over tomorrow after school so we can practice the whole show together."

"Yeah! I'll ask my parents tonight," I said.

"Me too," Isabel said.

I grinned at my friends. "This is going to be the best magic show *ever*."

Chapter Fourteen

Set It Up

When Chuck and I got home from school, I walked Banana around the block, ate a snack in the kitchen with Dad, then went to my room to practice the rabbit trick. Banana followed me up the stairs, bouncing with as much excitement as I felt. We were going to make magic!

During snack time, Dad and I had followed Sadie's suggestion and watched a video about how to pull a rabbit out of a hat. The video showed the same steps I had found in the magic book, but it was helpful to see them performed. I knew the magic stunt would be tricky to pull off, and I was eager to start practicing. If I could do it right, my trick would be even more impressive than Justin's. It would make Mrs. Shirley's birthday her best one yet.

I opened my library book to the correct page and placed it on the bed. "All right, first we need our magician's table," I said.

I cleared off my desk and pushed it toward the center of the room. Banana flattened her ears. She didn't like the noise of the desk's legs scraping the floor. I stopped pushing. "All done," I said to reassure her.

I stood behind the desk and checked that I could see myself in the mirror next to my dresser. I wanted to practice the trick while seeing how it would look to an audience, like the book had suggested. "We'll cover the desk with a tablecloth during the show, so no one can see under or behind it. But for now, just pretend the cloth is there," I said. Banana blinked and I knew she was picturing it.

I went to my closet and took out a bucket that used to be a beach pail. Now it held some of Banana's and my toys. I emptied it. "Isabel's going to bring me her dad's top hat tomorrow, but I can practice using this for now," I explained. Banana sniffed at the bucket and wagged her approval.

I spotted something shiny out of the corner of my eye, and went up on tiptoe to pull my glitter baton down from the closet shelf. Sadie and I had gotten matching batons a couple of years ago, before we met Isabel. I had never learned to twirl mine without dropping it, but now I had an even better use for it. It made a perfect magic wand.

I waved it through the air and the glitter inside it swirled and sparkled. Banana danced with excitement.

I put the bucket and magic wand on the table next to the black cloth Dad had helped me prepare for the rabbit. "The book says magicians pull rabbits out of hats instead of kittens or other small animals because rabbits are good at holding still.

They don't mind being in a pouch," I told Banana. "We'll have to handle Miss Fluffybutt very carefully, but I think she'll be cozy in this cloth."

I looked around my bedroom. "Now, what should we use for the practice bunny?"

Chapter Fifteen
Practice Makes Perfect

Banana's ears went straight up at the word "bunny." She ran out of the room. A few seconds later, she returned with her favorite squeaky toy, a yellow plastic rabbit, in her mouth. She bit down once to make the toy squeak, and dropped it at my feet.

I laughed. "Sure! We can use your bunny toy. Good idea," I said. I picked up the rabbit and placed it in the center of the black cloth. I wasn't sure how big Miss Fluffybutt would be, but since Justin had said she was a *mini* lop, I guessed the toy was probably only a bit smaller.

Banana watched as I lifted the four corners of the cloth together, so the rabbit was inside a little pouch. Dad had helped me cut holes in each of the corners, and I used those to hang the pouch from the knob on my desk drawer.

"We'll do this part of the trick when the audience isn't watching, of course," I said. "The setup happens *before* the performance. No one will know there's a rabbit behind the desk because the front of the desk will be covered."

Banana stared at the rabbit pouch. *She* knew

it was there, and what was inside it, too.

"Okay, here we go," I said. Banana sat. I stood behind the table and spread my arms wide. The Anna in the mirror did the same. "Welcome to the magic show! As you can see, there is absolutely nothing up my sleeves."

I picked up the plastic bucket and tilted it toward Banana. "This top hat is completely empty too," I said. I tossed the bucket into the air to prove how empty it was. It slipped through my hands on the way back down and landed on its side.

"Whoops. I guess I'll need to practice that part, too," I said. I threw it a few more times and focused on catching it perfectly. Banana thumped her tail against the carpet with each catch. Already I was getting better!

I put the "hat" on the table. "This is the tricky part," I said. Banana's eyes opened wider. "I'm going to pick up the hat and wave it around again. As I pick it up, I'll use my other hand to scoop up the rabbit pouch and put it *inside* the hat. The idea is to do it quickly and smoothly so nobody sees it happening."

I held the "hat" in my right hand, and used my left hand to lift the rabbit pouch and place it inside as I flipped the hat over. It felt a little clumsy. I did it again, watching my reflection in the mirror, and noticed the problem. I needed to lift the pouch right behind the hat if I didn't want people to see it. I tried it again. And again. And again. And again.

Banana watched closely every time. Finally, after so many practice-tries I'd lost count, I felt like I was getting the hang of it. I did it one more time, waved my wand in the air, said "Presto, Fluffybutt!" and pulled the rabbit out of the hat.

Banana went up on her hind legs to see it. I tossed the toy across the room and she ran to catch it. She trotted back happily and dropped the rabbit back into the hat. I knew what she was saying: *Again!*

Chapter Sixteen

Poof!

Banana and I practiced the trick a dozen more times, and I got better and better at it. Banana was the perfect audience. She always looked excited to see her bunny at the end. Each time I finished the trick, I tossed the toy across the room and she fetched it, brought it back, and dropped it into the hat. No matter how many times I did it, she always wanted to see the trick once more. We practiced and practiced until Dad called us downstairs to set the table for dinner.

When I got to school the next morning, Isabel

and Sadie were waiting for me. "I brought the hat!" Isabel called as I walked toward them on the playground. She pulled it out from behind her back and placed it on Sadie's head. Sadie giggled.

"I'm glad you finally got here. Isabel wouldn't show me her trick until you did," Sadie said. She

took off the top hat and handed it to me. I tried it on and it slid down over my eyes. It was too big for me to wear, but it would be perfect for the bunny.

"Show us!" I said.

Isabel dug what she needed out of her backpack. She stood and showed us a quarter in the palm of her hand. "As you can see, I have here an ordinary quarter," she said in a serious voice. Sadie and I looked at the coin and nodded.

Isabel used a square of paper to cover the quarter in her open hand. "I will now make the quarter disappear," she announced. She waved her other hand over the paper and said: *"Disappear-o coin-o!"*

She lifted the paper off her hand. The coin was still there.

My stomach sank, but Isabel didn't look too disappointed. "Oh," she said. "Sorry. Let me try that again."

She placed the paper back over the coin, waved her hand above it again, and said the silly magic words even more dramatically than last time: *"Disappear-o coin-o!"*

She lifted the paper. The coin sparkled in the sunlight. Isabel's shoulders dropped. "Whoops," she said.

Sadie and I glanced at each other. I wasn't sure what to say.

"It's okay, Isabel. Maybe you can—" Sadie said, but Isabel shook her head and interrupted.

"Let me try just one more time," she said. She put the paper back on her palm and waved her other hand in the air. *"Disappear-o coin-o! Poof!"*

she shouted. She squeezed her hand into a fist. When she opened her fingers, the paper was crumpled in a tiny ball, and there was no sign of the quarter.

Sadie squeaked in surprise. "Where did it go?" she said.

I looked down at the ground in case Isabel had dropped it. The coin wasn't there.

I looked at the crumpled paper in her hand. "Did you just *crush* the coin?" I asked. Isabel grinned and bobbed her head yes. "But how?" I asked.

She straightened out the paper ball and showed us the shiny foil inside it. "The coin was fake. I made it by covering a quarter with a circle of tin foil and rubbing it on the top and edges to make an impression. When I took the foil off the coin, it looked like a real quarter," she explained.

Sadie still looked amazed. "So those first two tries where the trick didn't work—you were just pretending?" she asked.

"Yup!" Isabel said. "Like Anna said, magic is a performance. I figured pretending to mess up first would make it an even better show."

"It definitely added suspense," I said.

"And made it extra surprising," Sadie agreed. "You really had us fooled."

"Speaking of fooling people . . . look," I said. I pointed across the playground. Justin was performing his magic trick for some kids gathered near the merry-go-round. He held up a card I couldn't see, but I could tell from the kids' faces he had guessed it correctly. I could imagine how smug *his* face looked.

I couldn't wait for my trick to go better than his. That rabbit and I were going to steal the show.

"One more day before we see his trick again," Isabel said.

Sadie nodded. "One more day, and we'll figure out his secret for sure."

Chapter Seventeen
So Many Secrets

The school day passed quickly, and soon it was time to board the bus to Sadie's house. Isabel and I gave the driver our permission slips and followed Sadie to the middle of the bus. It was Sadie and Isabel's turn to sit together. Sitting three to a seat isn't allowed, so I settled into the seat in front of them. I put the top hat in the empty spot beside me and opened my library book.

"Is that the hat for Miss Fluffybutt?" Justin's voice interrupted my reading. I looked up to see him peering over the seatback in front of me.

I closed the magic book so he wouldn't see what I was reading. "Yup," I said.

"Do you really know how to pull her out of an empty hat?" he asked.

I grinned. "I do."

"Awesome. Will you teach me?" Justin's face looked as hopeful as Banana's when she sees me eating a taco.

"Maybe," I said. "Will you teach me to do your card trick?"

Justin frowned. Before he could reply, the bus driver shouted, "Butts in seats! I need everyone facing forward before this bus can move."

Justin dropped out of sight. I didn't think he would say yes to the trade, but with luck—and Sadie's list—we might not need him to. I liked that he wanted to know *my* trick's secret, too.

Justin's stop came before Sadie's. He stood, gave me a quick wave, and said "See you tomorrow!" before bouncing off the bus. I looked out the window but didn't see any sign of Miss Fluffybutt.

When we got to Sadie's house, we went straight to the kitchen. I like going over to Sadie's dad's place because he lets us drink soda and always has tasty snacks. We never get soda at my house.

Sadie took three root beers out of the fridge

and put a bag of popcorn in the microwave. When the popcorn was popped, we brought it up to Sadie's room so we could share it while practicing our tricks.

The afternoon flew by like a turbocharged magic carpet. We practiced over and over, until our tricks went perfectly every single time. Soon I barely even cared about seeing Justin's trick again—I was too excited about everyone seeing mine.

Before we knew it, Isabel's grandmother had arrived to drive Isabel and me home. We climbed into Abuelita's minivan and buckled our seat belts.

As we pulled out of the driveway, I realized something. "Hey," I said. "We never finished our story about the tiny dragon who couldn't fly."

"Oh yeah! Where were we?" Isabel asked.

"The dragon just told the unicorn her embarrassing secret. The unicorn replied with a secret of his own, but we don't know what that is yet. It's your turn to add a sentence," I said.

"Hmm." Isabel tugged on her braid while she thought. "The unicorn told the dragon his secret, which was the secret to all magic: It only works if you believe," she said.

Abuelita smiled at us in the rearview mirror. I smiled back and added to the story. "The dragon closed her eyes and pictured herself flying across the mountain," I said. "She thought, 'I believe.'"

"When she opened her eyes, she realized she was flying," Isabel said.

"She could have been scared but she wasn't, because her best friend the unicorn flew beside her," I said.

Isabel grinned. "She'd discovered another secret: that friendship is magic, too. The end."

I couldn't wait to tell Banana the whole story.

Chapter Eighteen
Meet Miss Fluffybutt

The next morning, I woke up bright and early, too excited to sleep any longer. I leaned over the side of my bed and peeked at Banana. She was snoring softly in her doggy basket on the floor.

"Banana," I whispered. She opened one eye. "Today is the magic show!"

Both her eyes opened wide, and her tail thumped against her pillow in the basket. This was the day we'd been waiting for!

No one else in the house was awake yet. I brushed my teeth and put on my purple leggings and a black top with white glittery stars all over it. "How do I look?" I asked Banana. She twirled in a circle at my feet.

Banana and I practiced my trick again. I'd done it ten more times after dinner last night, and I did it ten more times now. "I've practiced so many times, I could probably do this in my sleep," I said.

Banana wiggled her whole backside. "You're right," I said. "That *would* be pretty funny."

I pulled her squeaky bunny toy out of the hat and tossed it across the room. She ran to fetch it, put her paws up on the table, and dropped it back in the top hat.

"The book says if you practice a trick enough times, your fingers memorize it. So even if your brain gets stage fright, your body will still know what to do. Just like magic!" I wasn't worried about getting stage fright, though. I couldn't wait to perform the trick for Mrs. Shirley with a *real* rabbit and make this her best birthday ever.

After a breakfast of pancakes for me and kibble for Banana, we helped my parents set up for the potluck. Mom and Dad carried my desk downstairs and put it in the living room, where the magic show would be. I covered the front and sides of the desk with a long dark tablecloth. I tucked my wand, the top hat, and the cloth that would hold Miss Fluffybutt on the floor underneath. I also put Mrs. Shirley's giraffe cards there, in case Sadie or Justin needed them.

Chuck helped me move Dad's favorite armchair to the perfect position for watching the show. It would be Mrs. Shirley's seat of honor— her birthday throne!

"I thought of another magic trick to add to the show," Chuck said.

"You learned a magic trick?" I asked.

"Not yet, but I'm sure I can do it," he said. From the mischievous look on his face, I knew a joke was coming. I narrowed my eyes and waited for the punch line. "I can saw you in half!" he said.

I put my hands on my hips. "*I'm* the magician, so I'll saw *you* in half."

Dad walked past us, carrying a giant bowl of

stew. "That's enough, you two," he said.

"What? It's a classic magic show trick! I'm offering to help!" Chuck said.

Dad rolled his eyes. "Why don't you help by finding the ladle for this chili?" he suggested.

Before Chuck could protest, the doorbell rang. Banana and I ran to open it. Sadie and Isabel were here! Banana barked to greet them.

They walked in followed by Abuelita, who carried a large casserole dish. "That smells delicious," I said. I took the dish from her and carried it to the long table we'd set up in the dining room.

The doorbell rang again and Justin and his parents came inside. Justin's dad held a dish for the potluck, and Justin was carrying a small plastic cage that Banana sniffed at eagerly. She wagged her tail the fastest I'd ever seen it go. I was excited to meet Miss Fluffybutt too!

I showed Justin, Sadie, and Isabel where I'd set up the table for our magic show. "This area is the stage. Mrs. Shirley will sit over there, in the seat of honor. The show will happen after dinner but before dessert. When our tricks are done, Dad will bring out the cake and everyone can sing 'Happy Birthday.'"

"Perfect!" Isabel said. "We can unroll our banner right before the show starts, so it doesn't give away the surprise." We'd made a banner yesterday that said MRS. SHIRLEY'S BIRTHDAY MAGIC SHOW. Sadie, Isabel, and I had decorated each letter with different colors and patterns. It looked really great.

"That's what I was thinking too," I said. "All

my props are set up under the desk. You can put your things there too. Sadie and Justin, I've got a pack of cards you can use."

"Thanks!" Sadie said, but Justin shook his head.

"I'm using my own cards," he said.

Sadie nudged me and winked. I knew what she was thinking. That might be a clue! If Justin couldn't use just any old cards, there might be something special about his deck or the way he'd arranged it. "Sure, no problem," I said. I kept my voice casual so he wouldn't suspect we were onto him.

Justin set the rabbit cage on the desk.

Unfortunately, he kept his deck of cards in his pocket. I was itching to get a peek at them. "Do you want to meet Miss Fluffybutt?" he asked.

"Yes, please! And I should practice the trick a few times with her too, so she knows how it will go," I said.

"Good idea," Justin said. He opened the little door on the front of the cage and an adorable, long-eared rabbit hopped out.

"Omigosh! She's so cute!" Sadie squealed. Miss Fluffybutt's nose twitched. She had round cheeks, bright eyes, and dark whiskers. She really was adorable.

Justin scooped up the rabbit and showed us the best way to hold her. "You cuddle her against you like this, and keep one hand under her butt to support it," he said. He held her out for Sadie to try. Miss Fluffybutt squirmed a little, then quieted against Sadie's chest.

"She's so soft," Sadie said. She stroked Miss Fluffybutt's ears with her free hand, then passed the rabbit to Isabel.

Isabel kept very still while holding her. Miss Fluffybutt held still too.

Banana sat close to my feet and watched as Isabel handed Miss Fluffybutt to me. Sadie was right: She *was* really soft. Her whiskers tickled my arm and I giggled. It was my first time holding a real, live rabbit and I loved her. But she was much, much bigger than I'd expected. And heavier, too.

"I thought you said she was mini," I said to Justin. "She's actually pretty big!" I was a little worried whether she'd fit comfortably in the hat. I was glad we had time to practice.

He shrugged. "I told you she likes to eat," he said.

I looked down at Miss Fluffybutt. She wiggled her nose at me. "Okay, well, we should practice a few times before the guests arrive," I said. But as soon as the words had left my mouth, the doorbell rang.

Chapter Nineteen

Let's Get This Party Started

My heart sped up and the rest of me froze. My friends and I looked at one another. Sadie and Isabel's eyes were as wide as Banana's. The guests were here already!

"Quick, put the bunny away," Sadie said. "We don't want the audience to see her."

I handed Miss Fluffybutt to Justin. He helped her into her cage, and tucked it under the desk where no one would notice her. Banana stuck her nose under the tablecloth to look, but I shooed her away. She ran to greet the neighbors instead.

"Now I don't get to practice with Miss Fluffybutt!" I whispered to Sadie and Isabel. I tried to stay calm but I felt super panicked.

Isabel put her arm around my shoulders. "You practiced a lot before this. We know you're ready."

Sadie nodded. "Don't worry, Anna. The show is going to be great."

I remembered the tiny dragon from Isabel's and my story, and felt a little better. *I can do it. And my friends will help me,* I thought. I just had to believe. But my heart was still beating quickly.

Justin grinned at all of us. "What are we waiting for? Let's eat!"

The house filled up

quickly with neighbors and food. Sadie, Isabel, Justin, and I piled our plates with everything we wanted to eat. I piled mine with a little extra to share with Banana when no one was looking.

Mrs. Shirley arrived, and I gave her a big birthday hug. "Thank you. How sweet of you to remember!" she said.

Banana danced around and I held my finger to my lips to remind her not to give away the surprise. "Banana says happy birthday too," I said. Mrs. Shirley bent down to pet her.

After I finished my dinner, I was too excited and nervous to keep still, so my friends and I helped with cleanup until it was finally time for the show. When most people's plates were cleared, Dad gave me a nod. I ran to the center of the room with Banana right by my side.

"May I have your attention, please!" I said in my best announcer voice. The room quieted down. "Please join us in the living room for a special surprise show!"

Chapter Twenty
Showtime

Banana led the way into the living room with her tail held high. The guests followed. They settled on the couch, in chairs, and on the carpet. Isabel guided Mrs. Shirley to the best seat in the house. "This chair is for you. It's the birthday throne!" she said.

"Oh my," Mrs. Shirley said. But she still didn't know what the surprise was. Nobody did! They were all watching and waiting to see what would happen next. My insides were jumping, just like Banana.

I told Banana to sit, then gave Sadie a thumbs-up. She held one end of the banner we'd made, and Isabel and I unrolled it. "Welcome to Mrs. Shirley's birthday magic show!" we said together, just like we'd rehearsed. The audience clapped and cheered.

I looked at Mrs. Shirley. She held one hand to her chest in surprise. "What on earth?" she said. Her face broke into a huge smile. I smiled back.

"I'd like to introduce our first magician: the magical, mysterious Miss Sadie!" I said. I swept my arm toward Sadie and she took a deep bow.

The rest of us moved offstage and Sadie stood behind the desk to perform her magic trick. She let Mrs. Shirley be the one to choose the card, and turned around to face the wall while Mrs.

Shirley showed it to the audience. It was the seven of hearts.

Sadie turned back around and did the whole trick perfectly—better than I'd ever seen it. When she lifted up the seven of hearts at the end and said, "Is this your card?" everyone gasped and applauded. Even Justin looked impressed. Sadie took another bow.

I stepped back into the stage area. "Please welcome our next magician: the magical, mischievous Mr. Justin!" I said.

Justin took Sadie's place behind the table. I stood off to the side with my friends. Sadie clutched my left arm and Isabel grabbed my right one. This was the moment we'd been waiting for! Our chance to figure out how the trick was done.

We watched carefully as Justin let Mrs. Shirley cut the deck and invited Chuck to shuffle. It definitely didn't look like Justin had the cards in a prearranged order. What else could the secret be?

Justin pulled a blindfold from his pocket, tied it around his eyes, and turned to face the wall. A neighbor from down the street chose a card, memorized it, and placed it back in the deck. Justin turned back to the audience and lifted his blindfold. Sadie, Isabel, and I all held our breath.

Banana stepped closer to Justin and tilted her head as he shuffled the cards. He placed them on the table, one by one, facedown, in a pattern that looked like a giant flower. My mouth fell open, and Sadie squeezed my arm harder. This was different from how Justin had done the trick last time. Was it a brand-new trick?

My heart did a cartwheel in my chest. Justin was fooling us again! We couldn't learn the secret of his trick because he'd tricked us by doing a new one! I had to admit that was pretty clever. I could tell Isabel and Sadie thought so too.

Justin placed the last card in the center of the flower, and flipped it over. "Is this your card?" he asked.

"Yes!" the neighbor who'd picked it answered.

"Amazing!" Everyone applauded, including Sadie, Isabel, and me, even though we felt disappointed. Justin's parents were clapping the loudest.

Isabel gave us a little shrug and went off to prepare her trick as Justin showed the card to the audience. It was the three of diamonds.

I gasped. Banana swiveled her head to look at me and lifted both ears. I nodded and she thumped her tail to join the applause.

I'd figured it out. I finally knew how Justin had done it!

Chapter Twenty-One
Fool Me Twice

I grinned at Justin while he took his bow. That was a pretty tricky trick he'd pulled. It had almost fooled me again, but not quite.

I couldn't wait to tell Sadie and Isabel what I'd figured out. But I would *have* to wait. We were in the middle of a magic show! And as my Nana always says, the show must go on.

I returned to the stage. "Our next magician is the magical, masterful Miss Isabel!" I announced.

Isabel stood in the center of the room to perform her disappearing coin trick. I ducked behind the desk and hid behind the tablecloth to prepare Miss Fluffybutt. Justin crouched beside me to help.

"Good job," I whispered.

"Thanks!" he whispered back.

"Say, can I borrow your deck of cards for a second?" I asked.

Justin narrowed his eyes. "What for?"

"Nothing much. Just to see if I'm right that *every* card in the deck is the three of diamonds," I said.

I could see from his face that my guess was correct. "How did you know?" he whispered.

I grinned. "Magic," I said.

Justin laughed, but softly, so as not to interrupt Isabel's trick.

"I knew it the second I saw the card," I told him. "I might not have remembered that we chose the same one, except that three is a very important number to me."

"You're not going to tell everyone, are you?" he asked. He opened Miss Fluffybutt's cage and took her out.

I shook my head. "Not everyone. Just Sadie and Isabel," I said. He looked like he wanted to protest, but there wasn't time to discuss it—we had to get my trick ready. It was almost time for the show's grand finale.

I unfolded the black cloth and Justin placed Miss Fluffybutt inside. I lifted the corners to make it a pouch, like I'd practiced with Banana's toy. But unlike all the times I'd done it before, this time the pouch was *moving*. It was heavier and larger now, too.

I looked at Justin in alarm. The book and video had said the rabbit would hold still for this part, but Miss Fluffybutt did *not* hold still. She squirmed and kicked, but Justin petted her and she settled down. I smiled my thanks. We hung the pouch from its knob.

"Don't worry. Sadie and Isabel know how to keep a secret," I said.

Justin frowned. He peeked inside the pouch to make sure Miss Fluffybutt was doing okay, and gave me a thumbs-up. I gave him a thumbs-up back, and the audience clapped loudly. Isabel had finished her trick. It sounded like it had gone just as well as the others. So far, our magic show was a huge success, and we'd saved the best trick for last.

I stood and placed the top hat and magic wand on the desk. Justin stepped aside to join the audience. I took a deep breath and looked at Banana for extra confidence.

It was time to make magic!

Chapter Twenty-Two
Faster Than a Speeding Bunny

Sadie stepped toward the center of the stage. "And now for our grand finale! The magical, marvelous Miss Anna!" she said.

Everyone clapped. I put the top hat on my head, holding on to the rim so it wouldn't cover my eyes, then tipped the hat toward the audience. I smiled extra big at Mrs. Shirley, and put the top hat back on the table. "As you can see, this is a perfectly normal, perfectly empty top hat," I said. I showed the audience there was nothing inside, then flipped the hat in the air and caught it, just like I'd rehearsed. Everyone clapped again. They were already loving it.

I lowered the hat toward the table with one hand. In my other hand, I grabbed the rabbit pouch, ready to lift it smoothly behind the hat like I'd practiced a million times. But it wasn't going the way it had in my rehearsals. Not at all.

The second I moved the pouch off the knob, Miss Fluffybutt squirmed inside it. I wanted to tell her "Shhhh" and "It's okay," but I couldn't say anything or the audience would see me talking to her. Instead, I held still, kept the pouch beneath the table, and smiled at the audience to pretend everything was okay. Miss Fluffybutt calmed down. I took a deep breath and tried again.

I lifted the pouch a second time. This time it

started smoothly. But just as I was about to drop her inside the hat, Miss Fluffybutt kicked at the sides with her giant feet and leaped right out of the pouch.

"Miss Fluffybutt!" Justin cried. A few people in the audience screamed in surprise, and others jumped up from where they were sitting. Miss

Fluffybutt shot across the room and ran past Banana, Sadie, and Isabel, straight behind Mrs. Shirley's chair.

Justin raced after her. He lunged to catch her but she darted out from under his grasp. "Miss Fluffybutt!" Justin called again. He jumped over the couch and chased her around the room as she ran in one direction, then another. I watched with horror. This was a disaster!

Everyone was standing and pointing or squealing. Miss Fluffybutt was on the loose and my trick was completely ruined. Chuck was laughing so hard, he had tears streaming down his cheeks. Sadie and Isabel were staring at Justin with their mouths wide open, like they couldn't believe what they were seeing. Even Mrs. Shirley was chuckling. I'd never felt so embarrassed.

Instead of pulling off the best trick ever, I'd become the biggest *joke* ever. And I'd ruined the big birthday surprise.

I picked up my glittery wand. I wished I could wave it through the air and fix this. But the wand wasn't really magic. I squeezed it in my hand and tried not to cry.

I felt a soft nudge against my leg and looked down to see Banana. She held the yellow plastic bunny toy in her mouth. She put her front paws on the table and dropped the bunny into the hat, just like she'd done all those times we had practiced. Then she lowered herself to the floor and sat, waiting for me to take the rabbit out of the hat.

I stared at her, then looked out at the audience. No one had even noticed what she'd done. Justin and Miss Fluffybutt had created the perfect diversion.

Banana swished her tail and I grinned at her. I knew just how to finish the trick now. Maybe the show wasn't completely ruined. Banana had saved the day!

"I got her!" Justin shouted from behind the couch. He stood, cradling Miss Fluffybutt in his arms. Everyone applauded, just like they'd clapped for his card trick—like this mixed-up, messed-up moment was a funny end to the show. But the show wasn't over yet.

Justin gave me a sheepish look. He hadn't wanted to steal my spotlight. "Sorry, Anna," he said. He kissed the top of Miss Fluffybutt's head.

"Don't be silly. I'm glad you caught your rabbit," I said. "But now, if I could have everyone's attention back, please—I was in the middle of performing my magic trick."

Sadie, Isabel, and everyone else in the room looked at me in surprise. They all thought my trick had been ruined. But not Banana. She sat up straight, watching and waiting. She knew exactly what was coming next.

I waved my magic wand over the top hat. *"Abracadabra, presto bunny rabbit!"* I said. I reached inside and pulled out Banana's toy. "Ta-da!"

Everyone gasped and applauded, even louder than they'd clapped before. I squeezed the bunny once to make it squeak, then tossed it high in the air. Banana jumped and caught it.

I'd pulled a rabbit out of the hat after all. Magic!

Chapter Twenty-Three

The Grandest Grand Finale

Justin, Miss Fluffybutt, Isabel, and Sadie joined Banana and me at center stage so we could take one more bow. When the applause ended, Dad stepped into the room with the final surprise: a birthday cake glowing with candles.

We all sang "Happy Birthday" and Mrs. Shirley wiped a happy tear from her eye. She clasped her hands together, made a wish, and blew out the candles with one big breath.

Dad cut the cake and I handed out the pieces. It

was chocolate cake with pink vanilla frosting: Sadie's, Isabel's, and my favorite. I let Banana have a small taste of the frosting. After all, she'd earned it with that trick.

"Were you surprised?" I asked Mrs. Shirley.

"Goodness, yes," she said. "You made my birthday wish come true! A party with a real magic show. Who would have thought? And I dare say no one will *ever* forget that grand finale. Your version of the rabbit-in-the-hat trick beats out even the one I saw as a kid."

"It didn't go exactly as planned," I admitted. "There was a bit of a mix-up."

"I've seen both versions, and I thought this one was even better," Sadie said.

"Me too," Isabel agreed. "It was much more surprising."

"It was *definitely* surprising," Justin said. "I still don't know how you did it!" He petted Miss Fluffybutt, who he hadn't let go of since he'd caught her. Miss Fluffybutt twitched her nose.

"The secret is to practice, practice, practice," I said. "*And* to have a magic helper on your team, like Banana." My friends laughed. Banana wriggled proudly. She bit down on her rabbit toy to make it squeak, and dropped it in my lap. I tossed it across the room for her. She scampered after it.

"I'm glad you had a good birthday," I told Mrs. Shirley.

"I did." She winked. "The most magical birthday ever."

Acknowledgments

Thanks to my editor, Alexa Pastor, for improving this book with her magic touch. A tip of the hat to the whole team at S&S, which has done so much to support this show, including designer Laurent Linn, editrix emeritus Kristin Ostby, illustrator Cassey Kuo, and Audrey Gibbons, Katrina Groover, Martha Hanson, Justin Chanda, and Anne Zafian.

Three bunny hops each for Rooga and Jeff; a glittery wand toss for Sophia and Anna; a pinch of magic fart powder for the original Chuck; and appreciative applause for my first and best audience, Ati and Mama—each of whom has a few good tricks up their sleeves. Scratches between the ears for Little Night and Popper, the best rabbits ever.

And—*ta-da!*—a bouquet of thanks for you, reader.

Collect all eight books in the Anna, Banana series!

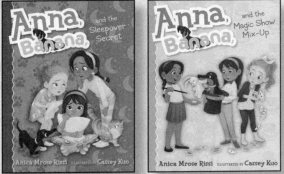